Welcome to ALADDIN QUIX!

If you are looking for fast, fun-to-read stories with colorful characters, lots of kid-friendly humor, easy-to-follow action, entertaining story lines, and lively illustrations, then **ALADDIN QUIX** is for you!

But wait, there's more!

If you're also looking for stories with tables of contents; word lists; about-the-book questions; 64, 80, or 96 pages; short chapters; short paragraphs; and large fonts, then **ALADDIN QUIX** is *definitely* for you!

ALADDIN QUIX: The next step between ready to reads and longer, more challenging chapter books, for readers five to eight years old.

Read more ALADDIN QUIX books!

By Stephanie Calmenson

Our Principal Is a Frog!
Our Principal Is a Wolf!
Our Principal's in His Underwear!
Our Principal Breaks a Spell!
Our Principal's Wacky Wishes!

Royal Sweets
By Helen Perelman

Book 1: *A Royal Rescue*
Book 2: *Sugar Secrets*
Book 3: *Stolen Jewels*
Book 4: *The Marshmallow Ghost*
Book 5: *Chocolate Challenge*

A Miss Mallard Mystery
By Robert Quackenbush

Dig to Disaster
Texas Trail to Calamity
Express Train to Trouble
Stairway to Doom
Bicycle to Treachery
Gondola to Danger
Surfboard to Peril
Taxi to Intrigue

Little Goddess Girls
By Joan Holub and Suzanne Williams

Book 1: *Athena & the Magic Land*
Book 2: *Persephone & the Giant Flowers*
Book 3: *Aphrodite & the Gold Apple*
Book 4: *Artemis & the Awesome Animals*
Book 5: *Athena & the Island Enchantress*
Book 6: *Persephone & the Evil King*
Book 7: *Aphrodite & the Magical Box*
Book 8: *Artemis & the Wishing Kitten*

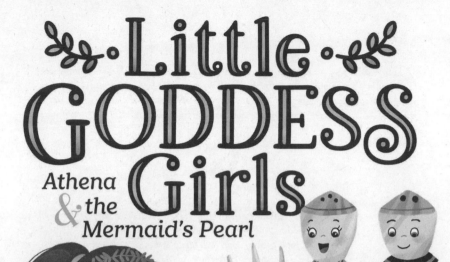

Little GODDESS Girls

Athena & the Mermaid's Pearl

JOAN HOLUB & SUZANNE WILLIAMS

ALADDIN QUIX

New Y... hi

ALADDIN QUIX
Simon & Schuster Children's Publishing Division
1230 Avenue of the Americas, New York, New York 10020
First Aladdin QUIX hardcover edition February 2022
Text copyright © 2022 by Joan Holub and Suzanne Williams
Illustrations copyright © 2022 by Yuyi Chen
Also available in an Aladdin QUIX paperback edition.
For information about special discounts for bulk purchases, please contact
Simon & Schuster Special Sales at 1-866-506-1949 or
business@simonandschuster.com.
The Simon & Schuster Speakers Bureau can bring authors to your live event. For more
information or to book an event contact the Simon & Schuster Speakers Bureau
at 1-866-248-3049 or visit our website at www.simonspeakers.com.
Designed by Tiara Iandiorio
The illustrations for this book were rendered digitally.
The text of this book was set in Archer Medium.
Manufactured in the United States of America 1221 LAK
2 4 6 8 10 9 7 5 3 1
Library of Congress Control Number 2021941919
ISBN 978-1-6659-0405-6 (hc)
ISBN 978-1-6659-0404-9 (pbk)
ISBN 978-1-6659-0406-3 (ebook)

Cast of Characters

Athena (uh•THEE•nuh): A brown-haired girl who travels to magical Mount Olympus

Amphitrite (AM•fih•TRY•tee): Mermaid goddess of the sea

Zeus (ZOOSS): Most powerful of the Greek gods, who lives in Sparkle City and can grant wishes

Hestia (HESS•tee•uh): A small, winged Greek goddess, who helps Athena and her friends

Oliver (AH•liv•er): Athena's white puppy

Artemis (AR•tuh•miss): A black-haired girl with a bow and arrow

Aphrodite (af•row•DIE•tee): A golden-haired girl with a chariot drawn by doves

Persephone (purr•SEFF•uh•nee): A girl with flowers and leaves growing in her hair and on her dress

Poseidon (po•SI•duhn): A walking, talking boy fork

Contents

Chapter 1: Mermaid Message   1

Chapter 2: A New Adventure   15

Chapter 3: No-Name City   30

Chapter 4: Poke!   48

Chapter 5: A Magic Spell   60

Chapter 6: The Pearl   76

Word List   81

Questions   85

Authors' Note   87

Mermaid Message

"Athena! Help!" a sweet, worried voice called out.

Eight-year-old Athena pushed her brown hair out of her face. Who was calling her name? She looked around the play area at

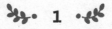

the shopping mall where she sat doing her homework. There were no people nearby. There was only the **mermaid statue** that stood in the middle of a fountain.

Statues can't talk, she thought. She must've imagined the voice.

It was after school. Her mom worked in the toy store across the way.

With a sigh, Athena finished her homework. After she put it in her backpack, she dropped it off with her mom, then came back out to the play area. Still no other kids around. Too bad. Hanging out with them would have kept her mind off her bad mood.

Why was it bad? Because she hadn't won the school invention fair today, that's why. Everybody always said she was super smart. Yet she'd come in second place.

Another girl had won. The girl's invention was a toy ship made out of a large soda bottle, partly filled with marbles. She'd built it so it wouldn't rock side to side very much in ocean waves.

Athena's invention was new seeds for plants that wouldn't need much water. They would help people grow food in places that didn't get enough rain. It was a good project, yet it hadn't won. You couldn't always win, she knew. But, still.

Just then, that voice came again. **"Athena! Over here!"** it called.

Athena's eyes got big. The

voice *had* come from that mermaid statue after all! She got up and leaned over the edge of the fountain toward it.

"Did you just talk?" she asked the statue.

Though it stood still, its mouth moved. **"Yes!** My name is **Amphitrite,"** the statue replied.

Huh? Magic like this usually only happened in a land Athena had been to called **Mount Olympus**. A storm had whirled her there the first time she went. However, she hadn't known that magic could leave that land and come here!

"Four **jewels** have gone missing from the tip-top of Thunderbolt Tower," Amphitrite went on.

Athena gasped. That was the tower in Sparkle City where **Zeus** lived! Zeus, a boy about her age, was the super-duper powerful king of the Greek **gods**. He could throw real thunderbolts! She'd met him on Mount Olympus a few times.

"Lost jewels?" Athena turned to study the play area. Since the mermaid had come to this mall, she must think the jewels ended up here, right? Before Athena could ask what *kind* of jewels to look for, Amphitrite spoke up.

"You won't find the jewels *here*. And they weren't lost. They were stolen!" the mermaid explained.

"Stolen?" said Athena. Her eyes went wide as she looked at the statue again.

"Mm-hmm. Zeus sent me here to ask you to help find them," said Amphitrite.

Oh! So that's why the mermaid came here—to find me! It pleased Athena that Zeus thought she could help. "Well, I can try. Do you have any idea who might have stolen your jewels?"

"**Yes!** The Four Winds stole

them! They're brothers," said Amphitrite. "But only one of the jewels is mine. The other three belong to other magical creatures."

Athena started walking back and forth, thinking. "I need more clues. What kind of jewels are they?"

"Well, the North Wind stole my black **pearl**," said the statue. The East Wind stole a green **emerald**. The South Wind stole a red **ruby**. And the West Wind stole a twin-kly **diamond**."

Athena nodded. "I'm guessing

they hid the jewels in different places around Mount Olympus?"

"Yes. And the jewels aren't just pretty," Amphitrite added. "Each has a special power. Together, their magic powers give Sparkle City its **sparkle**. Without the jewels, it's gray and foggy there now."

Athena stopped walking and stared at the statue. "Oh no! That's terrible. So, is Zeus too busy trying to fix the fog to also have time to find the jewels? Is that why he needs my help?"

"That's right. **Uh-oh! Gotta go**," the mermaid said. "I can magically travel to anywhere there's a mermaid picture or statue. Only for ten minutes at a time, though. Until the jewels are found, I can't swim in the sea."

"That's too bad," said Athena. She began to ask a new question.

But the statue spoke in a rush now. "One last thing—a secret. The four jewels also fuel Zeus's thunderbolts. Without the jewels, he's powerless to protect Sparkle

City! If those wild wind brothers find out, they might huff and puff until Mount Olympus blows away! For the jewels' magic to work against them, you must—"

Before the mermaid could finish, her words were cut off. The statue's lips quit moving.

Athena stepped closer to the fountain. "**Wait!** I must *what*?" But Amphitrite didn't answer. Her ten minutes were up.

Athena thought fast. She had made three friends on Mount

Olympus. Seeing them again would be fun. Time in that magic land moved much faster than here at home. So even if she were away a few days, her mom would still be at work when she got back. Her mom wouldn't even miss her!

She looked down at the golden sandals on her feet. Each had a white wing at the heel, and straps that crisscrossed up to her knees. They were magic! They'd become hers during her first trip to Mount Olympus. There, a fairylike

goddess named **Hestia** had told her how they worked. Now she clicked both heels together, and said:

"Magic sandals, whisk me high,
To Mount Olympus, I will fly."
Whoosh! She was whisked away!

2

A New Adventure

Minutes later, Athena stood on the Hello Brick Road. It was made of orange, blue, and pink bricks, and led to places all over Mount Olympus. There were flowers, bushes, and trees along it.

Unlike back home, it was early morning in this magic land. At the top of Mount Olympus, Athena could hardly see Sparkle City. Usually, its rainbow sparkles gleamed brightly in the sun. But the city was now covered in gray fog, like Amphitrite had told her. The pointed tip-top of Thunderbolt Tower poking up out of the fog was all she could see! **Woof! Woof!** Athena turned to spy a cute little white dog with a red collar. It was bounding toward her across a field of daisies.

"Oliver!" she shouted happily. "I've missed you." She had always wanted her own dog, but at home she wasn't allowed to have one. Oliver had become her pet here in this land, though. She kneeled and hugged him, rubbing his ears. Afterward, he ran around in circles, barking happily.

"Glad to see me?" she asked, giggling.

"**Yes!** We've all missed you," called a girl's voice.

"**Artemis?**" Athena jumped up to see her three friends. They'd appeared from between some trees. Now they were coming toward her on the road from Sparkle City.

Artemis grinned. "Yay! You're back!" She flipped her long black braid over one shoulder. As usual, she carried a bow and a **quiver** of arrows. She loved animals and took care of Oliver while Athena was gone from Mount Olympus.

Behind Artemis were two more girls. One wore a small crown atop her golden hair. **Aphrodite!** Beside her was a girl with flowers and four-leaf clovers growing in her red hair. This was **Persephone**.

All four girls rushed together in a group hug. "I'm sooo happy to see you!" Athena said. Her heart lifted as she and her friends smiled at one another. It felt great to be together again.

Though they'd only met a few weeks ago, they'd had lots of adventures since then. During the first one, Hestia had told them they were goddesses! They were all still learning more about how to use their goddess girl powers.

Aphrodite pointed down the

road behind them. "Did you notice how foggy Sparkle City looks?" she asked Athena. "We were heading that way to check it out when Oliver ran off."

"And now we see why he did," Persephone said with a grin. "He realized you were here!"

"Exactly," said Artemis. "But is there a reason for your visit? Do you know something about what's happening in Sparkle City to make it so gloomy?"

Athena nodded. "I do! Follow

me, and I'll explain." Quickly, she led them away from Sparkle City. As they walked along the road, she told them everything the mermaid had said.

"We need to get those jewels back," Athena said. "And hope that the winds haven't already guessed what powers they have. Or how to use those powers to make more trouble."

"Right. Those wind brothers are sneaky and like to tease. They're always blowing my hair around and messing it up." Aphrodite patted her pretty hair.

"Yeah," said Artemis. "Sometimes they blow my arrows off course when I shoot at targets."

"But they do good things too," added Persephone. "When they blow, it helps spread seeds around to grow new plants."

After a while, the girls came to a tall post. Beyond it, the Hello Brick Road split into three roads. One of the post's three signs read: NORTH. Another read: WEST. A third sign had both SOUTH and EAST written on it. Each sign pointed in a different direction.

"South *and* east? How can *one* road go *two* directions?" Athena wondered aloud.

The three signs spun on their tall pole, then stopped. **"Easy peasy!"** the pole told them. A talking sign pole didn't seem strange to the girls. Because in this magic land, many objects could speak!

"The south and east road circles around behind Sparkle City. Along the way, it splits in two," the pole went on. "One road goes south. One goes east. The city stands in the middle of all four roads."

"Think we'll find one wind brother at the end of each road?" guessed Persephone.

"Makes sense," said Athena. "Should we split up? If we don't, it will take four times longer to find all the winds."

Aphrodite started to speak. But suddenly, Oliver dashed off down the north road, chasing a butterfly. **"Wait, you silly puppy!"** Athena called. She zoomed after him, her sandal wings flapping. "I guess I'm going north! I'll look for the mermaid's black pearl there!" she shouted back to her friends.

Aphrodite cupped her hands around her mouth. "Let's meet up in Sparkle City after our jewel hunt!" she called.

"Okay!" Athena gave her a thumbs-up. Before going separate ways, the girls all waved goodbye.

When Athena caught up to Oliver, she picked him up in her arms. Then she looked back toward her friends once more. Artemis was walking down the west road. Aphrodite and Persephone were together, going down the road that went both south and east.

She crossed her fingers that their gifts would help them all succeed in their quests to find the jewels. During their first adventure, Zeus had given Persephone the gift of good luck. He'd given Aphrodite the gift of likability, and Artemis the gift of bravery.

Athena's magic sandals were her gift. They hadn't come from Zeus, though. They had found *her*.

Athena wished that she and

her three friends hadn't had to cut short their time together. But she was sure they'd soon meet again in Sparkle City. Having found all four of the missing jewels, she hoped!

With the help of her winged sandals, she sped off.

3

No-Name City

Athena zoomed north, flying inches above the road. Sometime later, she heard voices. People were coming toward her from a crossroad. She settled to the ground and put Oliver down.

It was easy to make friends on the Hello Brick Road, she knew. All you had to do was say "hello" to someone you met.

"Hello, I'm—" she began as three figures caught up to her. Then her mouth dropped open in surprise. Because now she saw that they were a giant fork, knife, and spoon! Each stood a bit taller than her. And all three had **arms, legs, and faces**!

"Um...hello," she began again. The knife cut off the rest of

what she'd been going to say. "Looks like you're headed for No-Name City, like us," it told her.

"I am?" Athena replied.

"Yes. It's up ahead," said the spoon. It pointed toward a big gate at the end of the north road. It was the entrance to a city.

Just then, a baking pan rushed by. It was holding hands with a pair of scissors.

"Hey, you shouldn't run with scissors! **It's dangerous!**" the spoon called to them.

The scissors frowned back. "Stop trying to stir up trouble, Spoon!" The pan and the scissors kept running. When they got to the gate, they went into the city.

Whoosh! A cold wind blew through Athena's hair and clothes.

It had to be the North Wind! Because . . . *brr.*

Hey! If the North Wind lives here, maybe it has hidden the mermaid's pearl close by, Athena thought.

The cold wind didn't seem to bother the fork, knife, and spoon. Probably because they were made of metal, unlike her!

Just then, Athena's stomach growled. She was super hungry. To her surprise, a plate of sandwiches suddenly ran by. One sandwich blew off in the wind. Oliver caught it in his mouth before it hit the ground, and ate it in a few bites.

Another sandwich blew off. **That was lucky!** Maybe a bit of Persephone's good luck had rubbed off on her when they'd hugged earlier? Athena grabbed the sandwich midair and started to munch. PB&J. *Yum!*

"Thank you!" she called after the plate.

"You're welcome," it called back. This north land was so

strange. The people who lived here all seemed to be dishes, cooking **gadgets**, and cookware. That could walk and talk!

She looked over at the large fork walking alongside her as she ate.

"So, what's it like being a fork?"

"Fork? I'm *not* a fork!" it grumped. "I'm a boy **trident**! My name is **Poseidon**."

Right then, another plate came along. It heard and rolled its eyes. "'Trident' is just a fancy name for a giant fork with three prongs," it said.

The knife gave the plate a sharp look as it rolled past. "Mind your own business!"

And the fork . . . er . . . *trident* yelled, "Yeah! Nobody asked you!"

Wow! This knife and fork could use Aphrodite's gift of likability! Because they weren't acting very nice.

As Athena, Oliver, and the others neared the city gate, she read the sign above it. It said: WELCOME TO NO-NAME CITY. A pair of tall salt and pepper shakers with gold tops stood guard at the gate.

"Who are they?" Athena wondered aloud.

"The queen and king of No-Name," said two chopsticks

who had caught up to her. They were twins! "The queen is the one wearing a sparkly gold necklace," said one. "She's the salt shaker. And the pepper shaker with the long purple cape is king," said the other.

"Why doesn't your city have a name?" Athena asked.

"It *does*! Its name is No-Name," the spoon replied.

"That's not a very good name," said Athena.

A candy dish heard her. "She's

right! There should be a contest to choose a better one!"

"Sharp thinking!" said the knife. "I'll go tell the queen and king."

"No, I will," said Poseidon. They raced ahead, each trying to be first to suggest the contest.

"Wait for us!" called the dish. When the dish ran

away with the spoon, Athena was left behind. She followed the others to the gate, Oliver at her heels.

"Not so fast, Fork," the queen told Poseidon when he reached the gate. "There's a speed limit in our city."

"I'm a *trident*!" Poseidon huffed. Then he and the knife told the queen and king about the contest.

"Excellent idea! We'll do it." The king smiled and waved them and some other dishes in through the gate. Oliver sneaked in with them.

The north road ended at the city. So it seemed likely to Athena that this was where the North Wind had hidden the mermaid's pearl. However, when she tried to pass through the gate to look for it, the pepper shaker king stopped her.

He bent close and asked, "Dish, cooking gadget, or cookware? Which are you?"

"I'm none of those," Athena answered. Suddenly she felt a

sneeze coming on. The king had accidentally sprinkled pepper on her! "Ah . . . ah . . . *achoo!*"

The king leaped back in surprise. "If you're none of those, then you don't belong here. Goodbye," he said. **"Next!"**

Oh no! Athena thought fast. What would her friend Artemis say right now? Something brave and bold!

"**Wait!** I'm . . . I'm Athena the, um, pitcher," she announced. Of course, she wasn't the kind of pitcher that poured juice. But she *did* often play pitcher on her neighborhood baseball team.

Too bad the king and queen didn't appear to believe her. Quickly, she put one of her hands at her hip. Then she bent her other

elbow like a
handle, and
pointed
her fingers
to look like
a **spout**.

"She does look
more like a
pitcher now,"
the salt shaker
queen told the king. Nodding,
they waved Athena through.

Hooray!

4

Poke!

Once Athena was inside the city, she searched for Oliver. Everywhere she looked, she saw more walking and talking dishes, gadgets, and cookware. Most were about her size. And there were walking and talking tables, ovens, and cupboards, too!

Being in this city was like being inside a giant, fancy kitchen, she decided. A kitchen where everything could speak and move around on its own!

Athena finally spotted her puppy napping under a table. *Good,* she thought. *He'll be safe there while I hunt for the pearl.*

News of a contest to rename the city was spreading. It had been decided that whoever invented the best gift for the city would win. The city would be named in their honor! But Athena didn't have time to think about inventions right now. She needed to find the mermaid's jewel!

However, everyone else in the city began inventing things in a hurry. A set of metal measuring spoons climbed onto a tree branch and hung itself from it. The wind made the spoons bump one another, causing a **musical** sound. *Clink, clink!*

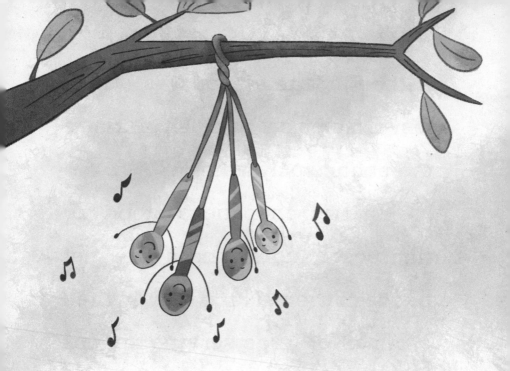

"Look! We just invented wind **chimes**!" the spoons exclaimed.

"I'll spice up this contest!" said a bottle of cinnamon. Quickly, it invented a new song called "How to Bake a Cinnamon Cake."

Although the song was really just a recipe set to music, it was a sweet and spicy tune!

The two chopsticks stood up like posts and strung a long net between them. Next, they invited a bunch of large serving spoons to hit a big ball of cookie **dough** back and forth over the net with their big round heads. "**Look!** We invented a new ball game called batterball!" shouted the chopsticks.

Meanwhile, Athena walked all

around the city looking for the mermaid's stolen pearl. Something that small could be hidden any- where! How would she ever find it?

She noticed that Poseidon appeared to be searching for some- thing too. Spotting a large muddy spot, that trident raced over to it. To her surprise, he dove headfirst into the mud. He landed upside down on his three-pronged head!

His prongs poked deep into the ground as his legs wiggled high in the air. After a minute, he pulled his pronged head back out and flipped himself right side up. He'd made three big holes in the mud.

"Three holes? That's your invention?" an ice-cream scoop asked him.

"That's just triple silly," said a frying pan.

"Wait and watch," said Poseidon. Everyone stared at the holes. Just then, a rumbling sound came from underground. "Stand back!" he yelled.

Suddenly, three fountains of

water shot out through the holes he'd made, going high into the air. *Splash! Splash! Splash!*

A cheer went up.

"Poseidon made a fountain!"

"Wow!"

"Amazing!"

"It's beautiful *and* useful," noted a bowl. "No-Name City didn't have enough water! Now we do!"

"Yes! And we can take a bath in it whenever we want to!" added a plate.

I guess dishes don't like to be

dirty, thought Athena. She had to agree, Poseidon's invention was the best gift to the city so far. But would it win?

"We can drink from his fountain too," said a cup. **"Hooray!"** A glass ran over and filled itself full of water. A straw hopped into the glass and took a big drink. Then its face turned red. It began to **cough**.

"Yuck! This is seawater," said the straw. "We can't drink it. It's too salty!"

"Salt is good for many things!" the queen said. She gave her own salt crystals a shake. "However, it is not good to drink. It's no good for watering crops either."

"Next!" said the king. *This meant Poseidon probably wasn't going to win*, thought Athena.

She felt sorry for him. She knew what it felt like to invent something cool, but see it lose in a contest. Quickly, she spoke up. "Salt is great to sprinkle on certain foods. Plus the fountain is pretty!"

"Yet, it's not what we need. So . . . nope," said the king. He and the queen moved on to look at more inventions.

5

A Magic Spell

Oh well, I tried my best to help Poseidon, thought Athena. She moved on too. She needed to find the mermaid's pearl! If she didn't, Sparkle City would stay gloomy. And the North Wind might find out the pearl had magic power and use it to play tricks on others! Where could that pearl be?

Hey! Could she come up with a magic spell to find it? Hestia had told her and her three friends to experiment with their goddess girl powers. That was the only way they'd discover how they worked.

However, Athena had once tried to put a spell on a boat she'd made for a science fair. To make it sail without wind blowing. Her spell hadn't worked. Still, that didn't mean a new spell wouldn't!

She thought for a few minutes. Then she closed her eyes and softly spoke these words:

Let the magic

of a goddess girl,

lead me to find

the mermaid's pearl.

Several moments went by. But nothing happened. With an unhappy sigh, she stuck her hands in her pockets. Her fingers touched something small, hard, and roundish. It felt like . . . **a**

pearl! Could it be this easy?

She pulled the object out. No, it wasn't a pearl. It was one of the seeds she'd invented, left over from her second-place invention.

Just then, something bumped her leg. It was Oliver. He had woken up and trotted close. The sudden b u m p surprised her, causing

her to drop the seed into the mud.

Crack! Athena jumped back in surprise as the ground by her feet broke open.

Whoosh! The seed quickly sprouted. It grew into a twenty-foot-tall tree with pretty green leaves. And it was loaded with things that looked very much like black pearls!

"But which one of them is the mermaid's pearl?" she wondered aloud.

"Pearl?" said the king. "I've

never seen a pearl tree before!"
He sounded excited.

Oliver started barking. He ran around and around the tree.

The queen clapped her hands happily. "We can use some of these pearls to decorate our crowns. The rest we can sell. Our kitchen kingdom will be rich!"

She turned to Athena. "You win the contest, Athena the pitcher!"

Poseidon ran over and pulled a pearl off the tree. He sniffed it and **squeezed** it. "Not so fast! These aren't real pearls. They're squishy and have a seed inside! Ha! They're worthless." He tossed it away.

"Look! If you squeeze one of these fake pearls, oil comes out," said the frying pan. "Oil is good for frying and cooking food."

"Oil can fuel a fire, too," said a mug. "For light. Plus its heat would keep my cocoa warm."

"Sounds great, but how does it taste," wondered the king. He popped one of the oily fake pearls into his mouth. Then he made a face and spit it back out. **"Ugh! Bitter!"**

The queen studied the pearls. "There must be some way to make them taste better. I know! Soaking them in saltwater for a month or more should do the trick."

Grinning big, Poseidon punched a fist high in the air. "Aha! Which means the salt in my fountain is good for something!"

"You're right," the queen agreed. "But *I'm full of salt*. The ocean is too. We don't need more. So Athena's invention is a more useful gift."

"Athena wins!" shouted the king. He turned to her and asked, "What is the name of your invention?"

"I don't know," Athena admitted. Just then, Oliver began digging under the tree until he found something among its roots. Something small and round. She bent

to look closer and gasped. Lying in the mud, was a *real* black pearl! It glowed with magic. The North Wind must have blown it into this mud to hide it! "Good job, boy! You found it!" she whispered. She gave him a hug. At the same time she sneakily pulled the pearl from the mud. As soon as she did, the cold North Wind started blowing harder. *Uh-oh.* It was trying to steal the pearl from her! Quickly, she tucked it safely into her pocket.

"I name the new tree I invented,

Oliver!" she said loudly. But the wind blew the last part of her last word away, so it sounded like she'd said "olive."

The pepper king spread his arms wide. "That's what we'll call it then. An olive tree!"

Athena didn't bother to correct him. *Olive* was a fine name for her invention! Once the black pearl was in her pocket, the North Wind seemed to give up. It stopped blowing around her. Instead, it went to play tricks on others, blowing sugar out of bowls and knocking napkins from tables.

"It's official!" shouted the queen. "We will name our city Athens, in honor of Athena the pitcher!"

Athena grinned big. Winning felt good! But she still felt sorry for Poseidon. She knew what it was like to lose a contest, after all. And his fountain *was* a great invention. So much water was spilling from it now, it was creating a beautiful new blue sea! "If only I had the magic power to make him feel better," she said to herself.

"Kindness is magic," whispered a tiny voice. It was the voice of the pearl in her pocket! And suddenly Athena knew how to help that trident.

She went up to him and smiled. **"Nice job, Poseidon!** You didn't only create a fountain, but a whole new sea! That's not something just anybody could do."

Poseidon looked very pleased by her words. "Thanks!"

Then she remembered that the

mermaid had said each jewel had a special power. The pearl's special power must be kindness! It had given her just the right words to help Poseidon feel better.

The king and queen had over-heard them talking. "Athena's right," the king said to Poseidon. "Yours is also a good invention."

The queen nodded, then announced, "We have decided that your fountain wins second place!"

Hearing this, Poseidon grinned even bigger. **"Woo-hoo!"**

Splash! He did a cannonball into his new sea and began to swim. Soon, dishes and other gadgets joined him, laughing and playing. It seemed that many others would enjoy swimming in his sea too!

6

The Pearl

Athena picked up Oliver and petted him. **"Good puppy!** We found the pearl, thanks to you. So I guess we're done here."

They left Athens through its city gates and began to walk along the

Hello Brick Road again. "I know someone else who would like Poseidon's invention," she told Oliver. "Amphitrite the mermaid. Maybe I could help them meet."

Oliver barked happily, as if he liked this idea too.

First, of course, she and her three friends would have to find three more jewels. And get those jewels back to Thunderbolt Tower. Only then would Amphitrite be free to swim in Poseidon's sea. And until then, Sparkle City would remain gray and gloomy.

At least they had found one jewel—**the pearl**! Athena wondered how Aphrodite, Persephone, and Artemis were doing with their searches. She felt in her heart that they would succeed too.

"I wish you all well, my goddess girl friends. See you soon," she whispered. She knew they couldn't actually hear her. Still, she hoped that wherever they were on Mount Olympus, they'd somehow *feel* her kind words. And that her wish would keep them safe on their quests.

No matter what troubles lay ahead for them, she knew they would do their very best to find the missing emerald, ruby, and diamond. She could hardly wait to meet up with her friends again and hear about their adventures!

"Time to go return this pearl," Athena said to Oliver. She set him on the road. Then she clicked both heels together, and said:

"Magic sandals, whisk me high,
To Mount Olympus, I will fly."

Flap! Flap! Oliver wiggled with joy. He knew what this meant, and he loved going fast! Grinning, Athena picked him up in her arms. Then the two of them zoomed down the Hello Brick Road toward Sparkle City.

Word List

chimes (CHIMZ): Bells, bars, or tubes that make a musical sound when they bump together

cough (KOFF): A sudden loud blast of air out of your mouth to clear your throat

diamond (DI•muhnd): A beautiful colorless jewel

dough (DOH): A claylike mix made of flour and liquid

emerald (EM•er•uhld): A beautiful green jewel

gadgets (GADJ•ets): Small tools

goddess (GOD•ess): A girl or woman with magic powers in a Greek myth

gods (GODS): Boys or men with magic powers in a Greek myth

Greece (GREES): A country on the continent of Europe

Greek myth (GREEK MIHTH): Stories people in Greece made up long ago to explain things they didn't understand about their world

jewels (JULZ): Beautiful costly stones often made into rings or necklaces

mermaid (MER•mayd): A magical woman with a fish tail that lives in the sea

Mount Olympus (MOWNT oh•LIHM•pus): Tallest mountain in Greece

musical (MYUZ•ick•uhl): Something that sounds like music

pearl (PERL): A beautiful jewel found inside an oyster

quiver (QWIV•er): A bag for arrows

ruby (ROO•bee): A beautiful red jewel

sparkle (SPAR•kuhl): Shine bright

spout (SPOWT): A tube that liquid flows through

squeezed (SKWEEZD): Pressed something between two fingers

statue (STAH•choo): A carved figure of a person or animal

trident (TRI•dent): A three-pronged spear

Questions

1. Imagine a magical creature you'd like to meet in Mount Olympus. What is it? If you could ask it three questions, what would they be?
2. The city of Athens, **Greece**, was named in honor of the Greek goddess Athena. If someone named a city after you, what might it be called?
3. What kind words would you say to a friend who hoped

to win a game or prize, but lost instead? If you lost, what would be the fair thing to say to those who won?

4. If you invented a special gadget to use in a magical kitchen, what would you call it? What would it do?

5. What special powers do you think the other three jewels might have? What adventures might Athena, Aphrodite, Persephone, and Artemis have as they search for more jewels?

Authors' Note

This book is a fun adventure twist on an old **Greek myth** that goes like this. Long ago, a city in Greece held a contest to see who could give its people the best gift. The prize? The city would be named after whoever won. The goddess Athena and the god Poseidon each tried to win. Poseidon poked the ground with his trident's prongs. Water whooshed up from the ground. But it was saltwater, which wasn't useful to the city. Athena invented the olive tree. Olives can be eaten, or squeezed to make cooking and fuel oil. And the olive tree's wood can be used to build houses, or as firewood. The Greeks were so happy with Athena's gift that they named their city Athens, in her honor. Today that's still the name of a real city in Greece!

We hope you enjoy reading all the Little Goddess Girls books!

—*Joan Holub and Suzanne Williams*